There Was an Old Fly Who Swallowed a Lady

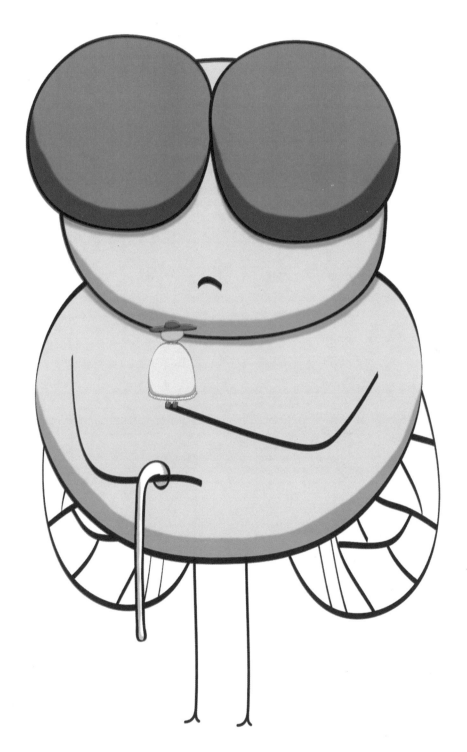

Written and Illustrated by Jason Pierce

ISBN 978-0-9850773-1-0

Published by 2Toad.
January 26, 2012.

For Sierra and Austin.
Love, Daddy.

There was an old fly
who swallowed some dirt!

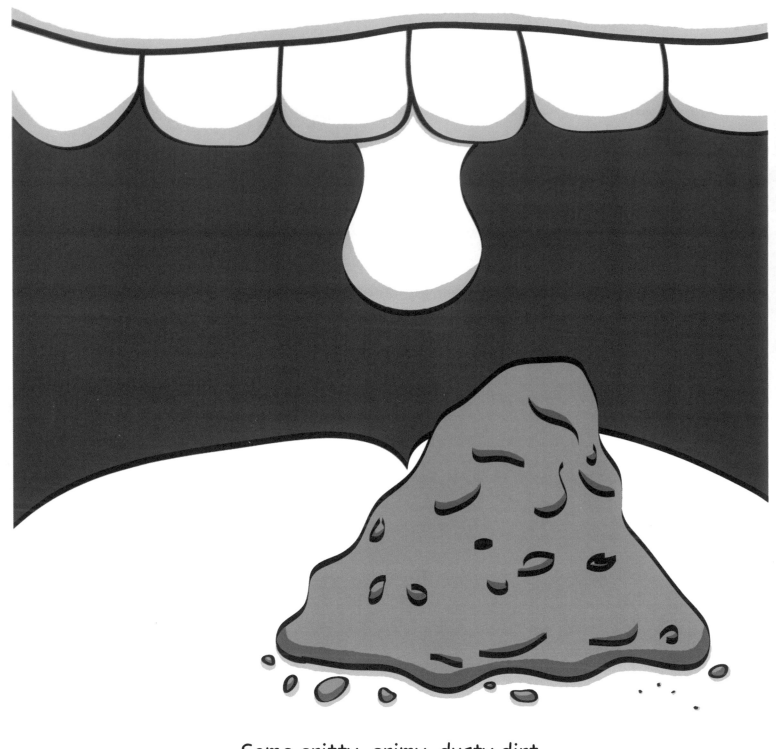

Some gritty, grimy, dusty dirt.

There was an old fly
who swallowed a worm!

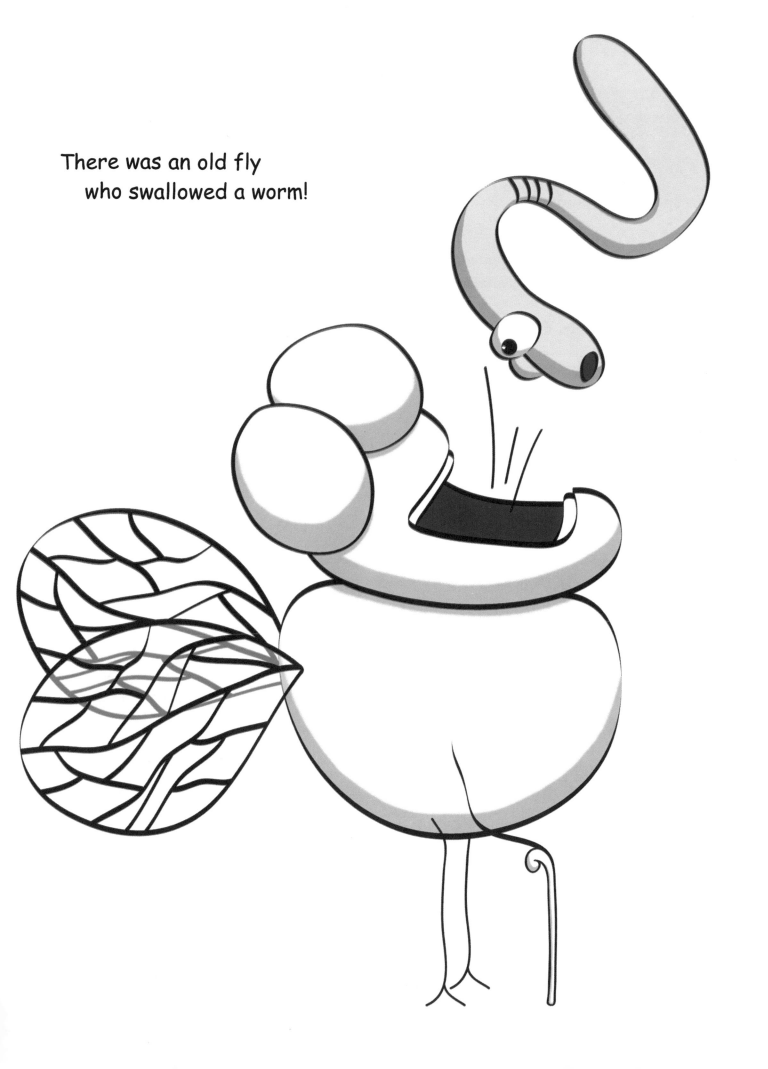

He swallowed the dirt
to attract a worm.

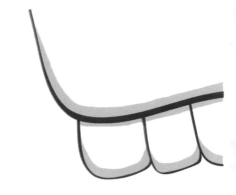

A slippery, slimy, wiggly worm!

There was an old fly
who swallowed a fish!

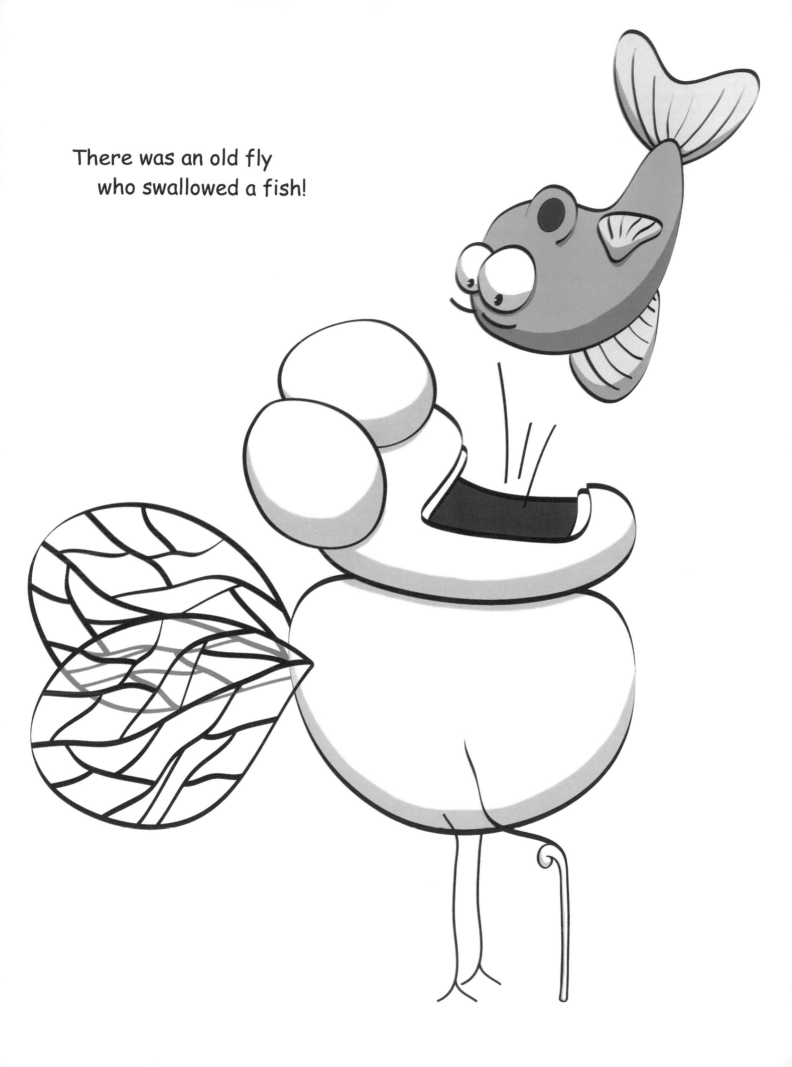

He swallowed the dirt to attract a worm.
He swallowed the worm to catch a fish.

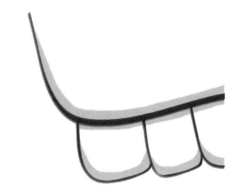

A scaly, smelly, finny fish!

There was an old fly
who swallowed a stork!

He swallowed the dirt to attract a worm.
He swallowed the worm to catch a fish.
He swallowed the fish to lure a stork.

FRESH FISH

A feathery, flappy, stilted stork!

There was an old fly
who swallowed a baby!

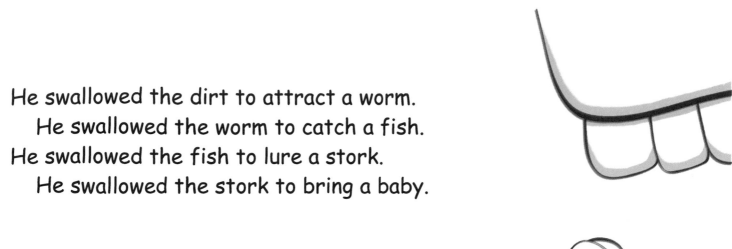

He swallowed the dirt to attract a worm.
   He swallowed the worm to catch a fish.
He swallowed the fish to lure a stork.
   He swallowed the stork to bring a baby.

FREE DELIVERY

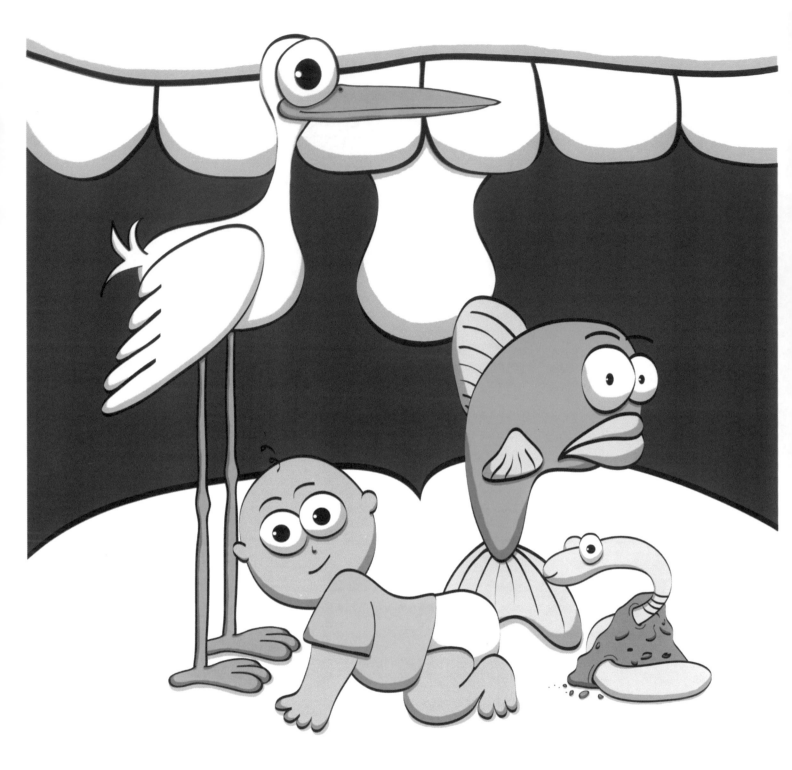

A cuddly, cute, bouncing baby!

There was an old fly
who swallowed a lady!

He swallowed the dirt to attract a worm.
   He swallowed the worm to catch a fish.
He swallowed the fish to lure a stork.
   He swallowed the stork to bring a baby.
He swallowed the baby to trick the old lady.

CUDDLY BABY

He swallowed the old lady...
to get revenge!

The End

Made in the USA
Lexington, KY
19 July 2012